## WILL CHELSIE AND HER MOTHER
## EVER GET ALONG?

Chelsie's attention was focused on the street where a long black limousine was pulling slowly to a stop at a red light. James was at the wheel.

As the limo idled, James turned and looked out the window. Straight at Chelsie.

Her heart stopped.

In the backseat, she saw her mother's face. She, too, seemed to be looking right at Chelsie.

Chelsie's throat tightened. Uh-oh! She was supposed to be grounded. And here she was sitting on a wall, eating hot dogs off the street, wearing what her mother might describe as a "ridiculous getup," and surrounded by girls her mother would think were "extremely unsuitable."

Her stomach flopped. Would her mother get out of the car and bustle Chelsie into the backseat like some kind of runaway delinquent?

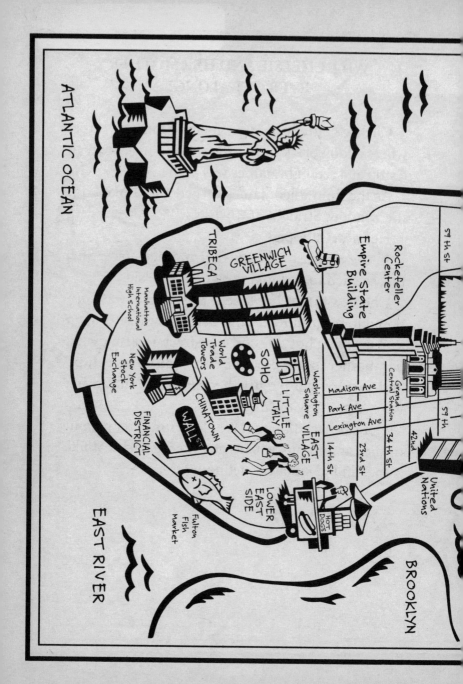

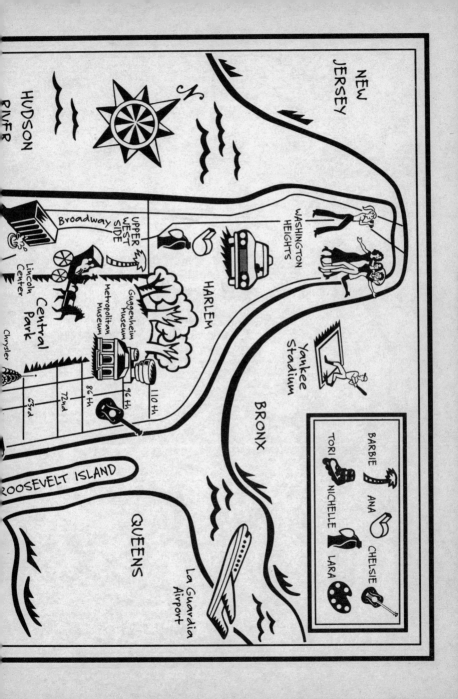

# GENERATI*N GIRL

#4

## Singing

## Sensation

By Melanie Stewart

A GOLD KEY PAPERBACK
Golden Books Publishing Company, Inc.
New York

A GOLD KEY Paperback Original

Golden Books Publishing Company, Inc.
888 Seventh Avenue
New York, NY 10106

GENERATION GIRL™ and BARBIE® and associated trademarks are owned by and used under license from Mattel, Inc. Copyright © 1999 by Mattel, Inc. All rights reserved.

Polaroid trade dress is used with permission of Polaroid Corporation.

Cover photography by Graham Kuhn.

Interior art by Amy Bryant.

No part of this book may be reproduced or copied in any form without written permission from Golden Books Publishing Company, Inc.

GOLD KEY is a registered trademark of Golden Books Publishing Company, Inc.

ISBN: 0-307-23453-3

First Gold Key paperback printing June 1999

10  9  8  7  6  5  4  3  2  1

Printed in the U.S.A.

# GENERATI*N GIRL

## Singing

## Sensation

# Chapter 1

# Leaving? *Again?*

"Well! Well! Well! I didn't expect you down this early, Chelsie. When I came in late last night, I heard you singing in your room."

Chelsie smiled sleepily, gave her father a kiss, and took her place at the breakfast table. "Why didn't you come in and tell me good night?" she said. "The whole reason I stayed up was to wait for you."

Mr. Peterson turned his mouth down. "Oh, dear. What a misunderstanding. I thought you might be composing and I didn't want to intrude upon you and your muse."

Chelsie giggled. "I think I can speak for my muse on this. You're always welcome."

Mr. Peterson made a little show of looking flattered, which made Chelsie laugh again.

There weren't many people who could make Chelsie laugh — but her father was one of them.

Mr. Peterson was cheerful, outgoing, and had a very silly sense of humor. No one would ever guess it to look at him. From the outside, he looked like a very proper British diplomat straight from central casting. He was tall, conservatively dressed, very distinguished, and surrounded by traditional English furnishings, traditional English servants, and traditional English traditions.

On the breakfast table, real English scones nestled in a linen napkin in a silver breadbasket. Three varieties of jam in crystal jars sat beside them, along with a small porcelain dish — (souvenir of the Queen's Jubilee) — full of fresh, clotted cream.

Alice, their English cook and housekeeper, managed to produce exactly the same kinds of meals they had enjoyed back home. Looking at the table, Chelsie found it hard to believe that they weren't still in England.

They weren't, though. They were in New York City, where her father was the new consul general.

Her father politely passed her the breadbasket. "So why *are* you down so early after a late night?"

"We have first-period assemblies on Monday mornings," Chelsie explained, deliberating over her choice of scone. "If I don't get there early, I'll wind up having to sit in the back with the Ravers."

"The who?"

"Oops — sorry. The Ravers are the kids at International High who are, you know, out there."

"Out . . . where?" her father said, furrowing his brow.

Chelsie smiled. Her father could speak French, German, Japanese, Hebrew, and four dialects of Chinese. He knew the appropriate greeting for every rank of royalty in every country. He understood what were — and were not — polite dining customs in every corner of the globe. And he could name the leaders of every country in the world, no matter how small or remote.

But when it came to the odd names and customs of I. H. students he was totally clueless.

Chelsie held back a giggle, wondering if she

could even begin to explain to her father the complicated differences between, say, the Bladers, who were pretty normal kids with a passion for in-line skating, and the Techies, the retro-hip nerds who had managed to build a renegade robot named Linus that roamed the halls of her downtown high school.

Bladers, Ravers, Goths, Techies. There were so many different groups of kids at I. H., it was hard to know where to begin.

"Oh, Chel-sieeee," her father sang. "Come back to Planet Earth. Your presence is requested at the breakfast table."

Chelsie realized her hand was still hovering over the silver breadbasket. She smiled. "Sorry, Dad. I drifted a bit."

He put the basket down and stroked her curly auburn hair, smoothing the crown. "Well, it's only to be expected," he told her fondly. "All poets are dreamers."

"Do you really think I can be a poet?"

"You are a poet."

"No. I mean a real poet. A grown-up poet. You know? Professional."

Her father thought for a second. "I'm not sure

4

that the publishing industry supports poetry in the way it should. So it's usually a hard go for most professional poets. But song lyrics are a form of poetry, and there are lots of professional song-writers. So I suppose the answer is yes. You could certainly be a professional poet."

Chelsie split her scone with a silver knife and helped herself to some clotted cream. She did love to write songs. Last year, in England, she had won the award for "Best Student Song." It was a ballad about homelessness — a subject about which Chelsie felt quite passionate. It was just as much a problem in New York as in England, she was dis-covering.

When Chelsie heard her mother's brisk, efficient footsteps approach the breakfast room, she auto-matically sat up straighter.

Chelsie's mom tended to disapprove of the way the kids in New York dressed and behaved. If she ever realized that the school actually had two young men known as the "Pants Boys" — because it was amusing to try and guess, on any day, whether their pants would actually fall off because they hung so low — she might insist that they all move right back to England.

Mrs. Peterson sat down at the breakfast table and smiled. "Good morning."

"Good morning, dear." Mr. Peterson rose slightly.

Chelsie sighed inwardly. Why did her parents have to be so formal all the time? They'd been married for almost twenty years, but her father always stood when her mother entered or left the room. And he always opened the door for her. He always said "please" and "thank you," and neither one ever raised their voice. Not to each other, and not to Chelsie.

Chelsie wondered what it would be like to have parents who every once in a while let their hair down and let everything hang out.

"What time is your plane today?" Chelsie's mother asked Mr. Peterson.

Chelsie's buttery scone turned to sawdust in her mouth. "You're leaving?" she cried. "I didn't know you were leaving. Why didn't you tell me?"

"Chelsie, please!" her mother scolded. "Not with your mouth full."

Chelsie did her best to swallow, but her throat was so tight, it took several big sips of the strong English tea to get the scone down.

Mr. Peterson dabbed at the corner of his mouth with his napkin. "I'm sorry, Chelsie. I just found out last night that I have to go to Portugal this evening."

"Do you have to go?" she asked in a small voice.

"I'm afraid so," Mr. Peterson replied.

"But I thought you were going to be home this month. We were going to rent horses and ride in Central Park. And . . ."

She saw her parents exchange a glance, and she closed her mouth, determined to say nothing else.

Mrs. Peterson's father had been a diplomat. She had grown up traveling the world. She clearly understood the duties and responsibilities that went with the job and with being a member of a diplomat's family. And at least once a week, it seemed, she subjected Chelsie to a long lecture on the subject.

The family hadn't come to New York on vacation, the lecture usually went. It had come to do important work on behalf of England. It wasn't fair to make her father feel guilty for doing his duty. It wasn't, well, *English.*

"I'm sorry," Chelsie said quickly.

Her parents exchanged glances again.

"Chelsie —" her father began.

Chelsie saw her mother frown slightly at her father.

Her father caught the look and abruptly changed the subject. Turning to Mrs. Peterson, he asked, "Are you sure you're up to handling the visiting delegations alone? I can put them off, you know."

"I won't be alone," Mrs. Peterson said, smiling across the table. "I'll have Chelsie to help me."

Chelsie munched at the edge of the scone, tasting nothing. Chelsie loved both of her parents, but she felt closest to her dad. Back in England, they'd gone to concerts and poetry readings and lots of plays. When they'd moved to New York, he'd promised to take her to some of the big musicals. They'd read the paper and made a list of the ones they wanted to see. Twice they had even bought tickets.

But then either the president came to address the U.N., or the South Americans called a special session, or something else happened in the world that required her father to go dashing off somewhere to fix it. It was always something. Chelsie's mom was almost as busy as Chelsie's dad. So the

Peterson home wasn't just a home. It was practically an embassy. At first it was exciting, but Chelsie rapidly learned that she could live in a crowded house, in a crowded city, on a tiny little island and still feel awfully alone.

Chelsie looked at her watch. The embassy limo always picked Chelsie and her father up after breakfast and whisked Chelsie off to school after dropping Mr. Peterson at work. The car would be arriving any minute. "Excuse me, Daddy," she said politely. "But look at the time. We'd better go."

"Oh dear, Chelsie," her father said, looking slightly guilty. "I am sorry. I won't be able to ride with you this morning. The Dutch ambassador is coming here. You run on and tell James to come back for me in an hour."

"All right," Chelsie said, disappointed. She quickly kissed both her parents and ran into the front hall where she had left her backpack next to the door.

She checked her appearance in the large, gilt-framed mirror that hung in the entrance.

All the other girls wore clothes that were funky, chic, retro, or just plain outrageous. Chelsie had a whole closet full of nice wool skirts, sweater sets in different colors, and sensible shoes. And she usually wrestled her curly hair into a neat braid that hung to the middle of her back. Chelsie wished that just once she could go to school in a pair of way wide pants, a halter top, and seventies-style platform boots. But she knew better than to ask. Her mother would probably freak out.

Outside, the long black car waited at the curb. Chelsie climbed into the back. "Good morning, James," she said politely.

James, the Petersons' driver, had come with them from England. He was very stiff, very polite, and very distant. He disapproved of American kids almost as much as Mrs. Peterson did. He folded his *London Times* paper and put it away. "Good morning, Miss."

Soon the glossy limousine was gliding smoothly down the broad Manhattan avenues and working its way west toward the Hudson River. As they neared the intersection of West and Warren Streets near Battery Park, a blue-and-gray-clad figure came streaking around the corner on a skateboard, narrowly missing the front of the limo by two inches.

James hit the brakes, and the limo came to a screeching stop.

The figure on the skateboard came to a stop as well.

Looking quite indignant, a tall, young woman wearing a helmet over her long blond hair stomped on her skateboard and sent it spinning upward. She caught it handily and tucked it under her arm.

"That young woman is going to get herself killed," James muttered in an irritable voice. "I'm going to tell her so." James rolled down the window. But before he could say a word, the young woman pushed her face into the window. "Hey! Boofhead," she barked. "Whyn't look where you going? An Aussie's not safe with a bloke like you swanking around the outback in a hearse like this."

James drew himself up. "Young lady, I have no idea what you just said, but your tone is very rude."

Chelsie burst into laughter.

The indignant young skateboarder's eyes darted toward the passenger seat. When they rested on Chelsie, the skateboarder's face broke into a bright, open smile. "Hello there, mate. Wouldn't have cracked a mental if I'd known it was you. See ya in school!"

And with that, Chelsie's friend Tori Burns dropped her board, hopped on, and skidded away.

Chelsie smiled. Tori was as close to a force of nature as a person could get. Strong-willed and fiercely independent, she had left her family behind in Australia to come to New York and live in Greenwich Village with her Aunt Tessa, an eccentric painter with a fascinating life story. Both Tori and Chelsie were sophomores at I. H. Both were fifteen years old. Both worked on the school newspaper and Internet web site. And both were members of Barbie Roberts's warm group of friends. Sometimes, though, Tori's colorful Australian expressions were as hard to understand as Chinese.

"Is *that* girl a friend of yours?" James asked scornfully.

Chelsie hesitated. James would be driving her mother this afternoon. She didn't want him complaining to Mrs. Peterson about her "unusual" friends. While none of her friends — Barbie, Ana, Lara, and Nichelle — was quite as out there as Tori, each had a strong, well-defined personality —

a personality her mother might easily misinterpret. If Mrs. Peterson thought Chelsie was falling into bad company, who could say what might happen? She might even try to send Chelsie back to England. Mr. and Mrs. Peterson had considered enrolling Chelsie in a "good English boarding school" just before they moved to New York. But Chelsie had begged them not to.

"No," she told James quickly. "She's not a friend. Just somebody I know from school."

She wished she didn't have to tell a half-truth. But by nature, she was shy and reserved. It was hard for her to express her feelings. She wished she could chill out, the way Tori and her other friends did.

All Chelsie really knew was that since meeting Barbie, with her sunny personality; Lara, with her wide-ranging intelligence and artistic sensibility; Ana, with her down-to-earth approach to life; Nichelle, whose good looks and fashion flair were a joy to behold; and Tori, with her wild and unpredictable personality, being a student at International High had become an adventure she looked forward to every day.

# Chapter 2

# Sing Out!

**T**he noise in the crowded auditorium almost knocked Chelsie over. International High had over three thousand students, and none of them was the silent type. Chelsie took a deep breath and plunged on in, moving down the center aisle along with all the other students who were scurrying to find a place to sit before the bell rang.

"*Allo!* Chelsie! Over here!" Chelsie spotted Lara waving at her from a row in the center of the auditorium.

Next to her, Barbie, Tori, Ana, and Nichelle

14

turned in their seats and waved enthusiastically. Tori pointed to an empty seat next to hers. "Saving this for you, mate."

"Excuse me. Excuse me," she said politely, squeezing past the feet, knees, and book bags that blocked her path.

*R-R-RING!*

Chelsie hit the seat the moment the bell rang.

Instantly, the auditorium hushed. Students at I. H. were allowed to do lots of things that weren't allowed at other schools. But the key to keeping their privileges was respecting the rights of other students and the teachers.

Mrs. Simmons, the school's principal, stepped up to the microphone and gave everyone a smile. "Good morning and welcome. Today, I am pleased and proud to announce the beginning of a new tradition."

Chelsie and her friends exchanged eager, surprised glances. "What does she mean?" Lara asked in her European accent that seemed to be part French, part German, and part Italian.

"Not sure yet," Tori whispered.

"As you probably know by now, we in the I. H. administration are firmly committed to education in the arts. We don't only value science, math, and history here. We also value creativity and self-expression. At I. H., music, writing, and art are not educational *frills*. We believe they are absolutely crucial to *all* learning. I know that many of you listening to me today will wind up pursuing scientific and technical careers. But I also know that many of you will not, because your talents lie in other directions. We want you to know that what you have to offer is every bit as important. And so," she continued, barely containing a smile, "I'm proud to announce that this year marks the first annual I. H. SING OUT!"

Barbie looked at Chelsie with big, bewildered blue eyes. "Sing *what?*" she whispered. Chelsie just shrugged.

"In case you're wondering," Mrs. Simmons explained, SING OUT! is a very special arts competition."

"Crikey!" Tori exclaimed.

"An *extreme* competition," Mrs. Simmons added, grinning.

"Double crikey!" Tori added.

Now Mrs. Simmons was smiling broadly. "I'm talking freshmen versus sophomores versus juniors versus seniors in a winner-take-all competition for best musical written, directed, and performed by a class. Winners get a Saturday trip on a Circle Line tour boat all around Manhattan Island. They'll have the boat all to themselves."

The courteous listening portion of the assembly was now over. The entire auditorium erupted into cheers, applause, and excited chatter — and there was no going back.

Mrs. Simmons shouted into the microphone, smiling at the students' excitement. "All interested parties — singers, dancers, writers, actors, artists, directors, stage managers, jugglers, mimes, extroverts, and introverts — report to your battle stations. Freshmen will meet in the boys' gym, sophomores in the girls' gym, juniors in the cafeteria, and seniors in the library. You'll have this period and next to get started."

Chelsie had no sensation of standing up and moving. She seemed to be floating toward the exit on a human wave. She wasn't even sure her feet were touching the ground.

As soon as the group turned the corner, the crowd began to separate. Most of the kids — the ones who weren't interested in participating — went back to class. The rest headed toward their respective meeting paces.

Chelsie, Barbie, Lara, Ana, Tori, and Nichelle struggled to keep together in the mob.

"Take your seats. Take your seats," Mr. Toussaint shouted as the kids poured through the doors of the gymnasium and into the bleachers.

Mr. Toussaint was the best English teacher in the school. He was also the sophomore class adviser as well as the faculty adviser to *I. H. Generation Beat*, the school newspaper and web site. He was a tall, very dignified African-American who reminded Chelsie of her father. Students who didn't know him sometimes mistook his proper dress as a sign of stuffiness. Nothing could have been further from the truth. Mr. Toussaint loved kids and loved teaching. He knew how to command students' respect while maintaining their trust. Best of all, he loved getting his kids involved in writing projects.

The students fell immediately silent. As Mr. Toussaint opened his mouth to speak, Barbie's hand shot into the air.

"Yes, Barbie?"

Barbie stood up and turned slightly so that she

could be heard by all the kids sitting behind her. "I just wanted to remind everyone here that the sophomores have a secret weapon." She paused for maximum effect. "We have a professional song-writer — *Chelsie Peterson.*"

Chelsie felt her face turn bright red.

"*Phmmlp skmmk mphoopm hmdif,*" said one of the Pants Boys down on the front row.

"I'm sorry?" Mr. Toussaint said.

"*Mmphx jomph kmmipms,*" mumbled the other Pants Boy by way of translation.

"I think he said he read about Chelsie and her songwriting award in the school paper," Lara offered helpfully in her thick European accent.

Both Pants Boys nodded and gave Lara a pleased and grateful smile.

It was quite odd. Nobody could ever understand a word the Pants Boys said. Very often, people had a hard time understanding Lara's accent, but some-how, Lara and the Pants Boys understood one another perfectly.

There was a lesson in there somewhere. But Chelsie had no idea what it was.

"I nominate Chelsie to write the songs," Barbie said.

The Pants Boys both raised their hands to second the motion. The next thing Chelsie knew, the whole room was applauding. Chelsie felt almost ill. She really wasn't sure she was up to the job. A musical?

What did she know about writing a whole musical?

Chelsie chewed nervously on a fingernail while the others debated who, what, when, where, and how the class would complete such a large project.

Fortunately, Mr. Toussaint was a master of organization, and before the hour was up, all the major production jobs had been assigned. Chelsie was asked to write the song lyrics. (Everybody agreed that to save time she should "only" write new words to existing show tunes.) Barbie was named director. Ana was put in charge of casting. Tori was assigned to write the script, Lara to design the sets, and Nichelle to create the costumes and handle the makeup.

Collectively, the girls were known as the Creative Committee.

When the special SING OUT! double period ended, Barbie paused outside the gym and motioned to all her friends to gather around. "I think step one should be a meeting of the Creative Committee — in someplace private so the other classes won't be able to hear our plans."

"Where?" asked Tori.

"How about at Chelsie's house? That way, she can play us her songs," Ana suggested.

Chelsie pictured in her mind all the polite, well-dressed men and women who would be sitting in the Petersons' living room — members of the French Delegation, the South American Delegation, the *Delegation of Delegations*. They'd all be speaking in soft voices and sipping tea from her mother's thinnest china cups.

She looked at her friends. How would her mother feel if she brought these rambunctious, uninhibited girls into the Petersons' tasteful and dignified home? *Not good*, Chelsie thought.

"Better not," she replied to Ana in her clipped English schoolgirl voice. "Mum's having people in."

"My place, then," Nichelle said. "After school. Chelsie can use my brother's guitar. I can't wait to hear her award-winning song."

"Oh, girls!"

The six friends looked up and saw Mrs. Simmons bearing down upon them with her son, Damian, in tow.

"Oh good-o," Tori muttered sarcastically. "It's Devil Spawn."

Ana and Nichelle choked on giggles. But Barbie, always poised, smiled at Mrs. Simmons and even at Damian.

"Girls," Mrs. Simmons said, "you probably all know Damian, right?"

"Mm-hmm," they all said.

"We've had the pleasure," Tori said wryly.

Damian was not exactly the nicest guy in the sophomore class. In fact, his nickname among his peers was Devil Spawn. But Mrs. Simmons was one of those people who was so nice herself, she never saw the faults in other people, especially in her own son.

"I was just talking to Damian, and it occurred to me that he'd make a wonderful production manager," Mrs. Simmons bubbled. "He's so organized! Have you filled that position yet?"

The girls looked helplessly at each other. They had never even thought of having a production manager. Mrs. Simmons had already drifted into the crowded hallway to answer questions from some excited junior girls.

Damian gave the girls a self-satisfied smirk. "I've had experience, too. At camp. With me in charge, we're sure to win."

Chelsie had no idea what to say. But Nichelle — never at a loss for words — spoke right up. "That's great," she said without missing a beat. "We'll probably be having a meeting sometime soon. So we'll let you know."

"Good!" Damian said. "I've got a lot of suggestions. So don't make any decisions without me." And with that, he dashed off to talk to a couple of skaters who didn't look very happy to see him coming.

*RRINNNGGG!!!*

The third-period bell rang, and the girls scattered in every direction. Chelsie was left standing in the hallway trying to collect her wits about her. As she headed for her locker, she almost began to wish her parents *would* send her to boarding school. The thought of having to perform her songs for everyone was almost more than she could stand.

# Chapter 3

# That's *Your* Opinion!

Nichelle opened the large oak door to her family's restored historic Harlem brownstone and let her friends inside. Chelsie and the other girls looked around with awe. The ceilings were at least fifteen feet high with elaborately scrolled molding.

A voice called from the kitchen. "Nichelle?"

"Mom?" Nichelle said with surprise. "Are you home?"

"Uh-huh, I'm in the kitchen. I left work early today."

Nichelle motioned to her friends to pile their

things on the window seat. "I've brought some friends with me, Mom. Come say hi."

Mrs. Watson came out of the kitchen and into the front hall with a large smile on her face. Chelsie immediately saw where Nichelle got the good looks that had made her a successful teen model.

Mrs. Watson was tall, slim, and dark-skinned, and she wore her hair in a braided bun. "Welcome," she said to the girls. "It's a pleasure to meet you."

While Nichelle performed the introductions and explained the larger purpose for the group's visit, Chelsie's eyes rested on a framed picture of Mrs. Watson with the mayor of New York, to whom she was an aide.

"An original musical!" Chelsie heard Mrs. Watson exclaim. "That's a very ambitious project. Isn't that going to cut into your study time?"

"*Mom!*" Nichelle protested. "We haven't even started and already you're making a fuss. It's not our idea. It's Principal Simmons's. It's all about valuing the arts."

Mrs. Watson lifted her hands in a gesture of surrender. "I'm hoping Nichelle never decides to be a lawyer," she said wryly to the other girls. "I haven't won an argument in weeks. If she changes her mind about careers and goes to law school, I'm sunk!"

The girls laughed, and Nichelle ushered them into the Watsons' comfortably furnished first-floor den.

"Here. This belongs to my brother, Shawn. He won't mind if we borrow it." Nichelle shoved a guitar into Chelsie's arms and then twirled around, plopping into a chair. "Okay." She grinned. "Let's hear this award-winning song."

All the girls sat down and gazed eagerly at Chelsie.

Chelsie perched on the edge of an ottoman and cleared her throat. She strummed the guitar and tightened the E string. When she was satisfied that the guitar was in tune, she tried to overcome her shyness by pretending she was performing alone in her own room.

"'The ache of life is in my bones,'" Chelsie sang, in her clearest soprano. "'Chilling strife. Jangling phones. Where is warmth? Where is peace?'"

Verse after verse described the unhappy faces and lives of people who had been made homeless by poverty, sickness, and family breakdown.

Finally, Chelsie strummed the last, minor chord

26

and sang the final, poignant line. "'Someone hold me, tight.'" She held the note for what seemed like an impossibly long moment, letting her high, bell-like voice fade slowly away.

When the last shimmering vibration of her voice ended, she heard a burst of applause.

Barbie and Tori beamed at her. But Chelsie noticed that Lara, Nichelle, and Ana seemed less enthusiastic. They were applauding, all right. But somehow they looked like they were just being polite.

"That's beautiful," Barbie said.

"Bonzer," seconded Tori.

Lara, Nichelle, and Ana exchanged glances. There was a long silence. Finally, Lara spoke. "But it is so sad, *non*?"

Nichelle nodded. "I agree. Now don't get me wrong," she added hurriedly. "It *is* a beautiful song. But it's . . . well . . . so down and so dark."

"A little depressing," observed Ana, casting her eyes down.

Anger flared in Chelsie's chest. "Life is depressing," she retorted.

There was another long silence. "How so?" Nichelle finally asked.

27

Chelsie's mouth fell open. Her friends were smart and sensitive. Could they really be completely unaware of the misery all around them? "Well . . . there are miserable people everywhere," Chelsie said. "I was thinking that maybe we could do our show about that."

Nichelle shook her head. "Remember what Mr. Toussaint always says," she said in a gentle tone. "It's always best to write about what you know. None of us are miserable, or hungry, or homeless. I think it would seem — I don't know — kind of pompous for us to write about an experience that we can't begin to understand. Let's face it. None of us has any reason to be too unhappy."

Chelsie's fingers felt numb. Her face felt cold. And her legs felt heavy. She was embarrassed that her award-winning song was not well-received. But, mainly, she was angry.

No reason to be unhappy? How about having the threat of boarding school hanging over your head? How about the reality of being constantly separated from the one person who really understood you? Just because she didn't babble morning, noon, and night about her feelings, why would her friends assume she didn't have any?

"I have to go," she said, standing abruptly.

"Oh, dear," Lara said. "We have hurt your feelings."

"No, how could you?" Chelsie replied tartly. "I don't have any, remember?" She put down the guitar, grabbed her backpack, and ran from the room.

"Chelsie! Come back!" she heard Nichelle shout. But Chelsie flew out the front door and onto the street. The subway stop was only a block away. She scrambled down the steps, thrust a token into the slot, and made it onto a waiting train seconds before the door shut and it went streaking downtown.

By the time she came out on the Upper East Side, her lips had stopped trembling and she was able to enter her house looking cool, calm, and collected — the way her mother always did.

Mrs. Peterson was in the front hall sorting through some mail. "Hello, dear. Someone just called you. Someone named Nichelle. Is she a friend?"

Chelsie's bottom lip shook, and she felt her face crumple. "No," she said, choking back tears. "I don't have any friends." And with that, she ran up the stairs to her room, threw her backpack down, and fell across the bed, sobbing.

Moments later, the door opened, and Mrs. Peterson

sat down beside her. "There, there," she said, patting Chelsie's back. "What's wrong?"

"I don't know," Chelsie choked. But she did know. What was wrong was that no one understood her creativity. Not her mother. Not the other girls. Nobody — except her father. And he was gone now all the time.

But she couldn't tell her mother that. She had to keep the traditional stiff upper lip. It was the English thing to do. Other kids could whine about not being happy, or not getting to do what they wanted to. But not Chelsie.

"Having a hard time fitting in?" Mrs. Peterson asked softly.

Chelsie nodded.

"These Americans!" Mrs. Peterson said. "They are not like us."

Chelsie sat up and accepted a tissue from her mother. "No," she agreed.

Her mother patted her back. "I'm sorry to leave you when you're upset," she said softly. "But I have to go to the African Delegation for tea. Would you like to go with me? I believe the Kenyan Ambassador has a daughter your age."

30

"No thanks. I think I'd rather stay home. Is that okay?"

"Don't you have *any* friend you would like to call? Someone to come over and keep you company?"

Chelsie shook her head. "No. I don't need anyone to keep me company. I'm going to write." She sat up and wiped her eyes. "I'll be all right," she said.

"Promise?"

"Promise."

Mrs. Peterson smiled. "Good girl. I won't be late. And when I get home, we'll have a long talk." Mrs. Peterson dropped a kiss on Chelsie's head. Somehow, her mother's tenderness made her throat tighten. "Don't hurry back," she murmured. "I'm fine."

She heard her mother descend the steps. As soon as the front door had shut behind her, Chelsie felt so lonely, she could hardly bear it.

She picked up her things and went into her father's study. Sometimes, when he was gone, Chelsie liked to sit at his desk and write. It made her feel closer to him.

The mail her mother had opened earlier was piled on top of the desk. When Chelsie pushed it aside, her eyes widened, and she drew in her breath with a gasp.

Right there, beneath some bills and a large enve-lope from the prime minister, was a letter from the Underwood Boarding School for Girls! That was where her mother had gone to school.

It was horrible to snoop. Almost a crime. But she couldn't help herself. She pulled the letter out and read it.

*Dear Mrs. Peterson,*

*We are delighted to inform you that a slot has sud-denly become available for your daughter, Chelsie. I know that you recently considered sending Chelsie to Underwood. If you are still interested, we could have a place ready for her in two weeks. Even though the semester has begun, I have looked over her excellent transcript and feel certain she will have no difficulty in catching up.*

*Yours sincerely,*
*Ms. Prunella Smythe*
*Headmistress*

Among the other letters on the desk was a plane ticket with Chelsie's name on it. She was booked in a seat for the 7:30 P.M. flight to London, leaving in two weeks on a Friday night.

*The very night of the show!*

"NO!" Chelsie gasped, tears springing back. "No. No. No." How could her mother do this to her? How?

*DING-DONG!*

Chelsie jumped, guiltily replacing the letter. Who could be at the door?

She ran downstairs, peered out the peephole, and saw her so-called "friends."

"Go away," she shouted angrily through the door.

"Let us in, please," Barbie pleaded.

"C'mon, mate," Tori urged.

"We want to talk to you," Ana said. "So quit acting like a little kid and let us in."

Chelsie reluctantly opened the door.

Barbie studied her face closely. "Wow! It looks like you've had a real cry, haven't you?"

"Girl, I feel terrible causing you to cry," Nichelle moaned.

Tori shifted her skateboard from one hand to another. "We're so sorry. It's not that we don't like your song. We do. You're bonzer talented."

"Mega-talented," Barbie added.

"Forget what we said," Nichelle insisted. "What do we know about songwriting? Our taste is in our mouths."

Chelsie shook her head. "I'm not crying about the song," she said chokingly.

"You're not?" Barbie blinked. "Then what's the matter?"

"My folks are sending me back to England to go to boarding school — on the night of the show!"

"They can't do that!" Barbie cried.

"Yes they can," Chelsie moaned. "And they will."

"But why?" Ana demanded.

"Because we're English. Because it's tradition." Very quickly, she explained how her mother and her mother's mother had attended Underwood. And how hurt she was that her father wasn't going to stop it. "I guess he just doesn't understand me as well as I thought," Chelsie said, trying to sound stoic.

"Maybe he doesn't know," Barbie suggested. "Didn't you say that the letter was addressed to your mother? And that it arrived today?"

Suddenly, Chelsie's heart soared. Maybe Barbie was right. Maybe this was all her mother's doing.

As soon as her father got home, Chelsie could get things straightened out.

"You're right," she breathed. "I'll bet when Dad gets home, he'll put a stop to it. No way would he let Mother send me back to England like that."

"There you go, mate," Tori said in a happy tone. "Problem solved, right? When's the old boy coming home?"

"Soon," Chelsie said, drying her tears. "As soon as he finishes this big trip he's on."

"Bonzer!" Tori said. "Then there's no reason to assume the worst. Especially when we need you so much for the show."

Chelsie's face brightened. She led her friends back upstairs to her room. Soon, they were deeply engaged in a discussion of what their musical should be about. Tori proposed a story about a group of daredevil kids, which was quickly rejected. Then Barbie suggested that the musical be based on the life of an important person.

"Wait, I've got it!" Ana exclaimed. "How about a show based on the life of Tori's Aunt Tessa? It's a great story. Young female artist falls in love, loses love, loses desire to create, and disappears for thirty years. Then, when her niece from Australia suddenly enters her life, she is persuaded to come out of hiding, and puts on a great show of her paintings. And nobody knows the story better than Tori."

"I-I don't know," Tori said.

"C'mon, Tori," Ana said. "You know it's a bonzer idea."

"Oh, all right," Tori said, smiling a little. "But I have to run it by Aunt Tessa — we don't want her to pack me off to Australia!"

"Yes!" shouted Ana. The other girls indicated their approval by pumping their fists and high-fiving.

"All right. Concept nailed," Ana said happily. "Chelsie? What do you think?"

"I think it's a fabulous idea," replied Chelsie. "But I'm not sure I know how to write something like that. You girls were quite clear that my style doesn't really fit the SING OUT! mood. I write pop ballads. I don't know many show tunes."

"So go to Recorded History, the music store, and ask for some major musicals," Barbie said. "Listen to them and figure out how to write in the show-tune style. You learn quickly. You can do it. In the

36

meantime, I'm going home to look at some old videos for directing ideas."

"And I am going to look at some of Tessa's paintings of the Southwest for set ideas," Lara said.

"Everybody start getting their act together," Barbie instructed. "Next creative meeting is tomorrow at Eatz. Be there, and be prepared to knock the juniors right out of the water."

The girls executed a silly, six-way high-five.

Then, suddenly, Chelsie froze. She heard a limousine door slam outside. "You have to go," she told her friends.

"What?"

"You have to go," Chelsie insisted. "My mum's home. If she finds you here, she'll . . . well . . . send me back to England, for sure. She doesn't want a lot of noise and disruption in the house."

"We're not noisy and disruptive," Tori and Lara exclaimed loudly.

"I know, but she'll think you are," Chelsie sputtered. "So it's the same thing. Please go or I'll get into trouble."

The girls jumped up. "Which way is out?" Ana whispered.

Chelsie hurried the girls through the front hall,

into the kitchen, and out the back door. "Wait until the car pulls away, then go round the corner and out the alley," Chelsie instructed.

"Looks like you've done this before," Tori said with a wink.

"Actually, I haven't," Chelsie admitted with a smile.

"You will," Nichelle assured her, disappearing around the corner along with the rest of Barbie's colorful crew.

# Chapter 4

# Chelsie's Style

"Excuse me." Chelsie timidly tapped the older salesclerk on the arm.

"Yes?"

"I wonder if you could help me. I would like to listen to the scores of some musicals."

"Which ones?"

"Well, ummm, I don't really know. I don't know very much about musicals. I'm trying to learn. Fast."

The clerk broke into a broad smile. "Come with me." He led Chelsie to the "Broadway" rack. "Here's *Gypsy*. I think it's the best all-round musical ever written. *My Fair Lady* — cleverest lyrics. *Sweeney Todd* — boldest concept."

Over the next half hour, Peter, the clerk — who also happened to be an aspiring composer and lyricist — gave Chelsie a whirlwind course in Musicals 101. She learned that a musical was not just a bunch of songs strung together. The songs had to help tell the story. And characters usually sang when their emotions were so big and overwhelming that they couldn't be expressed in mere words.

*I can get into this*, Chelsie thought happily as she paid for her CDs.

As she walked out the door, she saw a familiar figure. "Barbie!" she shouted.

Barbie glanced nervously back over her shoulder. When she saw it was Chelsie, her face relaxed.

"Something wrong?" Chelsie asked.

"I'm being followed."

"Huh? Who would be following you?"

"I'm trying to escape from Fletcher," Barbie whispered.

"Who?"

"Fletcher Minton. Mr. Toussaint let him sign up as my assistant. He's been following me all day. It's not that I don't like him, but he follows me so closely, he actually steps on my heels."

"Sounds like he's got a crush on you," Chelsie said.

Barbie smothered a giggle. "I'm afraid so. I can't think of any other reason why the president of the stamp club would develop a sudden interest in acting. But it's a one-way crush. I just don't want to hurt his feelings."

"So come on. Let's make a break for it," said Chelsie.

Barbie took Chelsie's arm, and the two girls ran around the corner and dashed into Eatz.

Tori, Lara, Ana, and Nichelle were gathered at a large round table in the back. They waved Barbie and Chelsie over. "Sit down," Tori invited. "We're just about to have a first reading of the script."

A friendly waitress placed a large platter of cheese fries in the center of the table.

"Ahhh!" Tori rubbed her hands eagerly together. "Food for creative thought."

"I can't believe you've already got a first draft," Barbie exclaimed, taking a seat.

"Well," Tori explained modestly while munching

on a cheese fry, "it's not like I had to make the story up. I just had to write it down. Aunt Tessa even helped. She said if we were weird enough to want to do a show about her life story, she might as well chip in. The hard part is going to be figuring out where to put the songs and writing the lyrics."

Chelsie felt her stomach clench. She was worried enough already. Over the next half hour, the girls laughed, shrieked, giggled, and made a thousand song suggestions as Tori read aloud the first draft of her script, entitled *Love What You Do*.

When she finished, all eyes turned toward Chelsie. "Well?"

"I think it's great." Chelsie put her hand on the stack of CDs. "Let me go home, do my homework, and then I'll get started on lyrics."

"In the meantime, I'll start blocking out the staging," Barbie said. Then she sighed. "Oh, no. Here comes Fletcher. He found me."

Fletcher came bounding through the restaurant in the direction of their table. He was extremely tall and extremely gangly. His long, narrow face wore a big smile. And his big feet seemed even bigger than usual. Maybe it was because he was wearing big, lug-soled boots.

When Fletcher realized the girls were watching, he began to "dance" in their direction, stamping his feet and trying to make rhythmic noises by kicking the surrounding tables and chairs.

Chelsie saw a waiter come hurrying in their direction, obviously prepared to put a stop to Fletcher's noisy display.

But before the waiter could reach him, Fletcher's foot snagged a chair leg and . . .

*YEOOWWWW!*

Fletcher yelped, tripped over the chair, and flew headfirst into the girls' table. The table tipped like a seesaw, and the remaining cheese fries flew up into the air and rained back down on Tori, who was seated on the other side.

The girls all let out shrieks of surprise, and the entire restaurant began to laugh and applaud.

Somehow, Fletcher managed to right himself, but his face was beet red and his eyes were miserable.

Chelsie felt sorry for him and held her breath.

Tori never hesitated to call someone a boofhead.

But before Tori could say a word, Barbie spoke up. "Whoaaa! Way to go, Fletcher. Funny bit. We'll definitely use that. Nicely done."

Fletcher's miserable face immediately cheered up.

Chelsie smiled. American girls might be outspoken, and occasionally rude, but they were nice. And they cared about people's feelings — which was more than she could say about her mother, she reflected bitterly.

"Gotta go," she said, remembering that her mother might get curious about where she was if she disappeared for too long.

"Do you have to go?" Nichelle protested. "I was hoping I could get your input on some of my costume sketches. Southwestern wear is really in fashion. Seems like lots of people would already have some stuff that looks right."

Chelsie looked down at her customary wool skirt and sweater. She shrugged apologetically. "Do I look like I would have anything useful to say about fashion?" She meant it as a joke, but her voice sounded rather angry — even to her own ears.

The girls all fell silent for a long moment. Then they began to protest her statement almost in unison.

" . . . you always look great . . ."

44

" . . . English style . . ."

" . . . very you . . ."

Their sputtering compliments only succeeded in convincing Chelsie of what she already knew: The girls considered her a fashion zero.

Oh, well. Her wardrobe was the least of her problems right now. She put some money on the table to cover her portion of the bill. "I've got a lot of listening to do," she said with a grin. "But just for the record, everything in my closet looks just like this."

"We can fix that!" Tori offered.

Barbie elbowed her in the ribs. "Chelsie doesn't need fixing," she said, glaring at Tori.

"Oh! Right-o!" Tori agreed immediately.

Chelsie choked on a laugh. How could she have doubted that these girls were her friends? They were all so supportive, so loyal, and so considerate of her feelings.

Twenty minutes later, Chelsie was entering the foyer of her Upper East Side home. She could hear the chatter of voices and the clatter of teacups and silverware against plates.

Her mother, hearing Chelsie enter, stepped outside of the living room. "Chelsie," she said happily. "I'm so glad you're home. Please come in and say hello to the French Delegation."

Chelsie felt anger flare up in her chest. How could her mother be glad to see her at home? She wanted her as far away as possible — in England.

Still, Chelsie could hardly make a scene with company present.

Chelsie stepped into the living room and smiled politely at the three ladies and four gentlemen. "How do you do?"

"Very well," a lady replied in an accent that reminded Chelsie very much of Lara's. "But tell us how *you* do. Such fun to be young and in New York City. So many interesting young people. Are you making many friends?"

Chelsie noticed her mother watching her intently, as if the answer was extremely important. Again, anger flared in Chelsie's chest.

"Ummm, I don't really have many friends," Chelsie said. "I'm too busy with my schoolwork and my writing." She indicated the stack of CDs. "In fact, I need to go listen to these right now. It's for a school project. It was nice to meet you."

Chelsie shot a look at Mrs. Peterson.

Mrs. Peterson dropped her eyes and stared at her nails. When she looked up, her eyes glittered — almost as if they were full of tears. But then, just as suddenly as they had appeared, the glittery tears were gone. "Very well, dear," Mrs. Peterson said in a kind voice. "Don't let us keep you."

Chelsie did her best to smile, shook hands all around, then ran upstairs to her room and shut the door. She was actually trembling.

*You can't get upset right now*, she scolded herself. *You have too much to do. You've got to listen to all these scores, and then figure out how to write one yourself. Father will be home soon. And when he gets here, he'll put a stop to the boarding school plan. He won't let her send me away. No way. No how.*

# Chapter 5

# The Plot Thickens

. . . One . . . two . . . three . . . four . . .

Chelsie hurried into the gym, where Nichelle was rehearsing a line of dancers. The dancers were portraying artists who lived in the Southwestern artists colony where Tori's Aunt Tessa had once lived and worked. It was the setting for the first act of the musical.

Barbie was filming the rehearsal with a digital video camera. It was her idea to tape all rehearsals, meetings, and backstage conversations. That way, the sophomores would have a running record of their experiences. Everybody thought it was a great idea, and Barbie was totally into it. She had the camera with her every hour of the day.

When Barbie spotted Chelsie walking in, she aimed the camera and approached her, speaking clearly to provide narration for the tape she was making. "Here is our award-winning lyricist and our secret weapon."

Chelsie couldn't help laughing, even though she didn't feel like anyone's secret weapon.

"Got any lyrics?" Tori asked eagerly.

Chelsie nodded, doing her best not to stare at the camera. She opened her backpack, fished around inside, and began handing out the lyric sheets to her new song.

"BONZER!" Tori cried happily, reading quickly. "It rhymes. It's funny. No, wait, scratch that. It's hilarious!"

Chelsie tried hard to conceal her pleasure. This really was one of her best efforts. It was set to the tune of an old song called "I Won't Dance, Don't Ask Me."

"You are brilliant!" Barbie said, laughing as she read the silly lyrics.

The song was a duet for the characters of Aunt Tessa and her parrot, Waldo.

"Show us how you see this," Tori said.

The group gathered around the table where Tori

had the music samples Chelsie had requested on a tape machine.

"Okay," Chelsie said shyly. "The parrot is very irritated with Tessa because she's not painting. And the parrot says, 'If you won't paint, I won't preen.'"

"So the parrot *sings*?" Tori gasped. "Crikey. What a funny idea."

Chelsie nodded. "Yes. Sort of like this." She pressed the button to play the music. As the music played, she began to sing the song in a silly, parrot's voice. "'I won't preen. Don't ask me. I won't preen, don't ask me.'"

When the first verse got laughs, Chelsie began to feel bolder about singing. She put one hand under her armpit so that she appeared to have a wing. Then she walked slew-footed — like a parrot along a perch — and flapped her arm to the music.

People began to laugh and applaud. Chelsie fought the urge to laugh herself. This was a new sensation for her — performing.

Nichelle began to imitate the step, urging her dancers to follow along. Soon, the entire cast was singing in a scratchy parrot voice, flapping their wings, and kicking up their "bird feet" to the beat. Carla Malay, the pretty singer who was playing

Aunt Tessa, threaded her arm through Chelsie's, and they began to dance together with the others forming a chorus line in the background.

"I love it! I love it!" Fletcher cried, going to town with his bird choreography. He twirled around, flapping his wings, jumped on the table and . . . .

*KABOOM!!!*

*CRASH!!!*

*SCREEEEE!!!*

The table fell over. The sound system began to shriek. And somehow Chelsie, Carla, Tori, and Barbie wound up in a pile, with Fletcher on top.

"Uhhhh, I think we might want to cut that last step," Barbie wheezed from the bottom of the stack.

"Oh, gosh!" Fletcher groaned. "I am, like, *sooooo* sorry."

There was a loud burst of laughter from the back of the gym. It wasn't nice laughter, either.

It was nasty laughter.

Chelsie struggled to her feet and squinted up into the bleachers.

"Spies!" Tori cried indignantly.

Sure enough, a group of about twenty juniors had been surreptitiously watching from the back.

"CLEAR OUT!" Tori yelled, scrambling to her feet. "YOU'RE NOT SUPPOSED TO BE IN HERE."

One of the juniors began to make silly parrot noises. "*AWWWK*. What's the matter, Polly? Scared of the competition?"

"Not likely," Tori retorted.

"You should be," another junior squawked.

Twenty juniors jumped to their feet, hopped gracefully onto the bleachers, and began moving in a perfectly synchronized dance step while singing a jazzy a cappella number about goofing off.

Out front were Jo Jo Hollander and Kingsley Feldman. Jo Jo and Kingsley were actual professional performers. Kingsley had been in two touring companies of *Annie*. Jo Jo had won all sorts of dance competitions.

Chelsie watched, torn between admiration and envy. The juniors were incredibly impressive. Openmouthed, she watched them switch over to a complex tap accompanied by a three-part hip-hop harmony.

Chelsie felt a wave of humiliation wash over her. What had she been thinking, she wondered, as she watched the juniors' professional and polished performance?

How could she have thought her material was anything like good enough?

She felt a hand settle on her shoulder.

It was Damian Simmons. "Don't worry," he whispered in an unpleasant tone. "Your production manager has a plan."

# Chapter 6

# Not Cricket

"What's Devil Spawn up to, anyway?" Tori asked grumpily.

The girls were in the corner of the gym that had been turned over to Nichelle for costumes. In the other corner, Damian was huddled with several girls and guys, including the Pants Boys.

"I don't know what Damian has in mind." Barbie sighed, executing an experimental pirouette with a denim skirt pinned loosely around her waist. "He's such a troublemaker. Let's be glad he's busy with some plan of his own and not pestering us."

"We don't need any 'plan' from Damian to win,"

Ana said. "We're going to win because we've got great choreography, great costumes, a great cast, and best of all, great writing."

Chelsie was grateful to Ana for her loyalty. But now that she'd seen what the older kids could do, she knew that her group had a huge job cut out for itself. "We can't win with what we've got right now," she confessed somberly.

Tori looked indignant. "What kind of talk is that, mate?"

"It's true," Chelsie replied. "We don't have a chance. We're kidding ourselves if we think we do."

"The direction is —"

"Fabulous," Chelsie interrupted. "But it could be better. The costumes are wonderful, but they're not as original as they ought to be. And my writing, so far, is way under par."

Chelsie watched the faces of her friends. She saw anger and confusion warring with the sneaking suspicion that Chelsie was dead-on right.

"Amazing the way the people who can't take it can dish it out," muttered Tori.

Chelsie's face reddened. "I'm sorry. I didn't handle the criticism well at Nichelle's house. I took it personally. But I shouldn't have. And now you shouldn't, either. We've all done good work. But if we want to win, we've got to do *great* work. And we can. I know we can."

"Be realistic, Chelsie. We can only do so much in two weeks," Ana argued. "And we've all got other things we have to do. Classes. Homework. Sports. The newspaper."

"Have no fear, the fixer is here!"

The girls turned around. Damian, Garrett Adams, and the Pants Boys hovered behind their little group.

"I couldn't help overhearing," Damian announced. "Chelsie is out to lunch, and Ana's right. We can't do better work than we've already done."

Chelsie felt a flutter of anger in her chest. *We who?* Damian hadn't done any work *at all.*

"The juniors have some really talented people in their class," Damian continued. "We can't win on talent alone. We don't have anybody like Jo Jo Hollander or Kingsley Feldman. Sure, Barbie's good. So are Carla and some of the others. But they're no Jo Jo and Kingsley."

"What are you saying?" Ana said sharply.

"I'm suggesting we level the playing field,"

Damian answered. "Maybe we make sure one or two of their stars don't exactly make it into the show. Stars who at this time shall remain nameless." He snickered at his own lame humor while his eyes darted around the group in search of approval.

Chelsie drew in her breath angrily. "That's not cricket!"

"You're right," Damian said with a smirk. "It's not cricket. It's show business."

"What do you intend to do?" Ana asked angrily. "Step on their toes or something? Break their kneecaps?"

Damian shook his head. "Nothing so crude. I happen to have a little inside info on Jo Jo's and Kingsley's ... ummm ... less than stellar math grades. Suppose my mom were to start getting notes from parents demanding that SING OUT! operate on a 'No Pass–No Play' basis. The juniors would lose their big stars because Jo Jo and Kingsley would be, as they say, benched."

There was a long silence as everyone digested the deeper meaning of this piece of information: Damian had been looking through his mother's

private student files. And if he had access to Jo Jo's
and Kingsley's records, he had access to *everyone's*
records.

"*Ttwdd chrttmng mmimophh momojop,*" muttered Pants Boy One.

"*Shlump hmph mimn msopp smill, mp mieel
wrmm joomph,*" muttered Pants Boy Two.

Ana, Chelsie, and Barbie exchanged bewildered
looks. Nichelle just shrugged. None of them had
any idea what the Pants Boys were saying.

Lara came to their rescue and provided the
translation: "Pants Boy One said, 'We can't do
that, it would be cheating.' Pants Boy Two said,
'Damian's plan is "a sword that swings two ways." A
lot of sophomores would be benched, too.'"

Barbie had something to say, too. She stepped so
close to Damian that her face was only two inches
from his. "If you even try a miserable thing like
that," she said, "I'll . . . I'll . . ."

"You'll what?" Damian challenged nastily.

"I will tell your mother," Barbie finished. "And
everyone here will back me up."

Damian's face colored angrily. "You wouldn't."

"Yes, I would," Barbie insisted. "And, further-
more, if you ever snoop into people's records

again, we won't just tell *your* mother, we'll tell *our* mothers. And then your mom will start getting a lot of notes from angry parents! And guess who's going to take the heat?"

"GRRRRR," grumbled Damian, storming off.

Gasps rippled through the group. This was truly a first. None of them had ever seen Barbie lose her temper. Like Principal Simmons, she always saw the best in people and always wanted everyone to get along. But she also had a clear sense of right and wrong. And, in this instance, she didn't mind letting Damian — and everyone else — know exactly where she stood.

All the sophomores standing around her broke into applause.

"All right, then," said Tori, clapping her hands. "You heard what Barbie said. We're going to do this show right. And we're going to do it fair. Even if it means" — she gulped hard — "that we stand no chance of winning."

# Chapter 7

# The Pressure's On

"Did you get those fabrics stretched?" Nichelle asked Marina Gray, the shy textile artist who was serving as assistant wardrobe mistress.

"Uh-huh," Marina confirmed.

It was Friday. Chelsie moved through the girls' gym where the sophomore crew was feverishly working on the costumes, sets, and dances that it hoped would make *Love What You Do* the best, hippest, and most sophisticated production I. H. students would ever produce.

"Got those new lyrics?" Melissa Larkin demanded, hurrying over to Chelsie. Melissa was in charge of making sure everybody in the cast had the most up-to-date version of the script.

Melissa was extremely short. Barely five feet tall. She was also a master of organization, and a chess champion.

Chelsie opened her folder and removed the latest set of lyrics to "Desert Dessert" — a funny group song-and-dance number in which Aunt Tessa cooks up cactus pie for twenty people.

"Hope this is the last revision," Melissa said, shaking her head over the large number of changes Chelsie had made.

"We've got a good cast," Chelsie said. "They'll learn the new lyrics fast."

Melissa nodded. "Okay. Just don't forget that as of Monday, the show is frozen. That means no more changes."

"No more changes," Chelsie promised.

Over the course of the week, Chelsie had spent hours in the I. H. library listening room. After she'd played her collection of CDs over and over, and read the scripts of several shows, the whole project had begun to make sense.

Every day, she and Tori went over the script, making it stronger, funnier, and more romantic.

Chelsie had come up with some fantastic ideas. One of them was to have a scene in which all the artists in the colony joined together to sing about the joy of painting. As they sang and danced, they would paint — right onstage! — the fabulous Southwestern scenery that would be the backdrop of the show.

Of all the songs Chelsie wrote, though, the one she liked best was a ballad about the difficulties of trying to create when the person you loved most was far away. The song was called "When You're Away." Chelsie hadn't shown the song to any of the girls yet. She wasn't sure she wanted to. It was moving, but it was also sad — just the kind of song that the girls had told her to avoid earlier. Still, she wrote the song because she felt it defined the heart of the show. Maybe next week, when they started full rehearsals, she would let them hear it.

"Chelsie!" a voice called out. Chelsie turned and saw Ana motioning her to come over to where she was working with Mike Haynes and some dancers. Mike Haynes was playing the role of Waldo, Aunt Tessa's parrot.

Ana drew Chelsie aside. "Mike says his throat is going. Doing that scratchy parrot voice is tough.

I'm going to let him play one of the painters and recast Blaine as the parrot. That okay with you?"

Chelsie nodded. "Of course. You're in charge of casting. Do what you think best."

Chelsie was flattered that Ana was asking for her opinion. She suddenly realized that her own heightened level of perfectionism had inspired the entire company. Everybody wanted things to be done right.

Ana made some notes on her clipboard and turned back to her group. "Okay, then. Let's try this number again. Fletcher!"

Fletcher looked over from the piano area where he was conferring with Barbie.

"Could you come and help me work out this number?" Ana asked.

Fletcher nodded. "Sure thing." He strode purposefully toward Ana, successfully navigating sawhorses, several props and pieces of set, buckets of paint, and a number of performers who were sprawled out across the gym floor doing stretching exercises.

Chelsie sat down on a bleacher and watched Fletcher prepare to lead the Pants Boys and the dancers through the scenery-painting number.

During the rehearsal, the dancers were only supposed to *pretend* to dip their paintbrushes in the bucket. Come the night of the show, they would actually paint the scenery.

"Wow," Ana murmured. "Have you noticed that everybody, including Fletcher, seems to be getting more professional by the hour?"

"I've noticed," Chelsie answered.

Fletcher pressed the button on the tape player. The intro music began. "One! Two! Three! Four!" Fletcher shouted, getting the dancers pumped for the athletic dance routine.

Chelsie watched with pleasure as the girls and boys moved expertly through the complicated steps. The music began to build. The dancing became more exuberant.

Excitement gripped the gym. People left their costumes, rehearsal groups, and construction sites to watch. They began to clap to the music. Melissa passed out lyric sheets, and several people jumped right in, singing along.

Chelsie couldn't sit still. She jumped to her feet. It was incredible. Just incredible. The scene was *working*. The voices, the dancers, the music, the words — everything.

# Singing Sensation

Fletcher, usually so clumsy and awkward, moved almost as gracefully as Barbie. He leaped across the gym, spun around, and held his brush poised over a bucket of paint.

Suddenly, Chelsie noticed that it was a *real* bucket of paint. Not a prop.

"No!" she cried out. But it was too late.

Fletcher dipped his brush into the bucket of sunset pink that Lara had mixed for the actual performance.

"*Non! Non! Non!*" Lara shouted as Fletcher went into a spin.

"*Mmmohpumimp holim umph,*" Pants Boy One protested as Fletcher's brush spritzed him with pink paint.

"*Imop ujmoohmph fumphwah,*" Pants Boy Two moaned as pink paint dotted his face and T-shirt.

Barbie, seeing the trouble, came running over, hit the button on the tape machine, and brought the music and the dancers to a stop. "Fletcher!"

Fletcher was so embarrassed, his face turned almost as pink as the paint.

"Fletcher!" Barbie said, wagging her finger at him. "How many times do I have to tell you? The Pants Boys do *not* look good in polka dots.

If you're going to decorate them, stick with stripes."

Everyone began to laugh, including the paint-splattered Pants Boys.

"Okay, take ten, everybody!" Barbie ordered. She dismissed the dancers and joined Chelsie in the bleachers.

"I'll find some paint remover and get this stuff off the floor," said Fletcher, hurrying away.

Barbie took a moment to catch her breath, then said to Chelsie. "Tell me honestly. Not counting this mess-up, how do you think we're doing?"

Chelsie looked Barbie straight in the eye. "You know, I'm actually starting to think we have a chance of winning."

"Only a chance!" Lara said, shaking her head. "I think we are a sure thing. Unless, of course, Fletcher sprays the audience with polka dots. Then, perhaps, we lose."

Ana giggled. "Lose the front row, you mean."

"I'm going to tell my mother to sit way in the back," Nichelle said with a grin.

"Speaking of parents," Ana said. "Both of mine are coming. So are my three aunts, four uncles, seven cousins, and a bunch of neighbors."

"Aunt Tessa said she wasn't going to come, at first," Tori said with a grin. "She was really uncomfortable when I told her we were making a musical out of her life story. But when she actually read the script, she said it seemed like a lot of fun and she'd be glad to come."

Chelsie listened to the girls compare notes as to who would be coming and who would not.

"I've got to go," she said, standing quickly, before anyone could ask her about her family. She still had not heard from her father. And she had no idea who would be coming on the night of the show.

She grabbed her pack, hurried out the side door, and then walked toward the bus stop.

It had been a hard week full of hard work. But the hardest part was feeling as if she were being spied upon at home. The cat-and-mouse game her mother seemed to be playing with her. The waiting game.

Every day, her mother would question her intently:

*Isn't there anyone you would like to invite over?* she would ask.

*Didn't James see you walking with some girls the other day?*

"No," she would reply. "I really don't have any friends."

Chelsie felt guilty about lying. But she had a horrible feeling that James was watching her and then reporting back to her mom that Chelsie was forming some very unsuitable friendships. When her father got home, Chelsie was afraid her mother might use her "unsuitable friends" as a way of convincing her dad to send her off to boarding school.

If only she could speak to her father.

As the bus carried her uptown toward her home on Embassy Row, Chelsie's stomach began to tighten in knots. If her father didn't get home soon, he might get home to discover Chelsie gone — back to England. Chelsie couldn't believe that her mother had said nothing to her yet about the letter. It had been days since it had arrived.

There was no way Chelsie could introduce the subject herself without revealing that she had read her mother's mail. That would be unforgivable.

Until Mrs. Peterson put her cards on the table, there was nothing Chelsie could do except make sure she gave her mother no reason at all to complain. Not about her behavior, her friends, her clothes, or even her room.

# Chapter 8

# Tea and Sympathy

"**M**y!" her mother exclaimed that evening when she came into Chelsie's room and saw Chelsie putting away all her socks, papers, and books. "What is all this about?"

Chelsie shrugged. "I had some time and I thought things were looking very messy. So I decided to clean up."

She watched her mother's face, hoping to see some sign of approval. Instead, her mother got that tight, slightly pained look she seemed to wear constantly now. "It's time for tea. Let's go downstairs. I want to talk to you."

Chelsie drew in her breath. Was her mother finally going to admit that she was trying to send her to boarding school?

Chelsie followed her mother downstairs and into the rather formal sitting room off the main receiving room. Tea was laid out on a side table. Small sandwiches were arranged on silver platters.

But Chelsie had no appetite and took only a cup of tea.

Her mother sat down in a high-backed chair and gave Chelsie a strange stare. "Chelsie," she said. "You're looking quite pale. Are you feeling well?"

*Fat lot you care*, Chelsie thought bitterly. Still, she forced herself to smile and sound chipper. "Yes. Quite well, thank you."

Mrs. Peterson took a sip of her own tea and cleared her throat.

Chelsie tightened her fingers around her cup. Here it came. In a way, she was relieved. Once her mother broke the news, then at least Chelsie could fight back.

Mrs. Peterson took a letter from her pocket.

Chelsie's heart began to thunder.

Mrs. Peterson put on her reading glasses and

appeared to peruse the letter again — as if she couldn't quite believe what she was reading. She folded the letter, put it in her lap, and then, gazing at Chelsie, said, "Are you quite happy at International High?"

"Yes!" Chelsie practically shouted.

Her mother bit her lower lip. "Is the work more difficult that you anticipated?"

"No!"

"Too easy, perhaps?"

Chelsie gritted her teeth, "No. It's just right."

"Then can you tell me why you have missed two math classes, a history quiz, and have failed to turn in your homework for most of last week?"

Chelsie felt the color drain from her face. *That wasn't the letter from Underwood. It was a letter from I. H.*

She knew she had been consumed by the SING OUT! project. But she didn't have any idea she was falling so far behind.

"I've been working on a school musical," Chelsie said quietly.

Her mother raised her eyebrows. "What?"

"I've been working on a school musical. Writing

lyrics. It was the principal's idea," she said, remembering the way Nichelle had dealt with Mrs. Watson's objections.

Mrs. Peterson pressed her lips together. "Am I to understand that the principal at International High considers a school musical more important than academics?"

Chelsie swallowed. Trust her mother to twist things around.

"No. I mean . . . yes . . . . well . . . this is special. It's a contest. It's about honoring the arts."

Mrs. Peterson frowned. "Honoring the arts is one thing. Permitting it to replace your schoolwork is another." She paused, then said, "Does this have anything to do with peer pressure? The need to please friends?"

"NO!" Chelsie protested, fighting tears.

The phone rang, and Mrs. Peterson picked it up. "Giles!" she exclaimed, her face lighting up. "I'm so glad you've called. How was Portugal?"

Chelsie clenched and unclenched her hands. How could her mother sit there talking to her father as if everything were perfectly all right when everything was just *horrible*?

"Yes . . . yes . . . yes . . ." Mrs. Peterson smiled.

"She's here." Mrs. Peterson handed Chelsie the phone. "Your father wants to speak to you."

Chelsie took the phone. "Daddy!" she cried joyously. "When are you coming home?"

"Not yet, darling," her father replied. "I've been asked to go to Egypt."

"But . . ."

"It's about something terribly important, I'm afraid. You'll be a good girl and forgive me, won't you?"

"But I want you to come home," she cried. "I've helped write a show at school. The performance is next weekend. I want you to be there, *Daddy*!"

"I just can't, pumpkin."

Suddenly, all of Chelsie's pain, anger, and hurt welled up in her chest. She began to sob. "You're never here when I need you. Never! And . . ."

On the other end of the phone, she could hear static and her father's distressed voice. "Chelsie. Chelsie, dear. Please."

Her mother, visibly upset, took the phone. "Giles, I'll handle this. Just call us when you can." Chelsie heard her hang up the phone.

She took Chelsie in her arms and tried to hug her. "Chelsie, dear. That wasn't fair. Daddy doesn't enjoy being away from us. But it's his job. He has a duty. A responsibility. Surely you understand?"

Chelsie twisted out of her mother's embrace. "I understand," she shouted. "I understand that nobody in this house wants me here."

"Chelsie!"

"I understand that I come last. Behind everyone and everything. Behind the French Delegation and the African Delegation and the Indian Delegation and —"

Her mother stood and cut her off. "Go to your room," she said wearily. "I'll bring you some tea."

Tea? *Tea?* Chelsie felt as if her life were ending, and all her mother had to offer was tea! "I don't want any TEA!" Chelsie bellowed.

"That is the absolute limit," Mrs. Peterson announced, angry now. "Chelsie, you are grounded. I want you home directly after school every day. Understand?"

"Sure, I understand," Chelsie said, glaring at her mother. "I understand more than you think."

And with that, Chelsie ran out of the room, up the stairs, and into her bedroom where she SLAMMED the door and locked it.

# Chapter 9

# A Day to Remember

Chelsie had heard her mother giving instructions to James this morning. Mrs. Peterson would be leaving with the Indian Delegation, visiting a traveling exhibition of Indian dance and art in Midtown, and then showing them around New York. It would be late that afternoon before she returned home.

Chelsie left the house quietly. Outside, she buckled on her in-line skates, then went whizzing through the sunny New York streets, setting a course for Eatz, downtown.

The girls were all gathered in the back of Eatz. It was one of the few restaurants around town that didn't make a fuss about skates. On Saturdays, the girls all wore them. It was cheaper and faster than taking the bus or the subway.

In the back, at a large, round table, the girls laughed and giggled, but as soon as they saw Chelsie's face, their own faces turned sober.

After a night of sobbing, Chelsie's was pale and puffy.

"What's the trouble?" Tori asked.

Quickly, Chelsie related what had taken place yesterday afternoon. How it looked as if her father wouldn't be getting home in time for the show — or, more importantly, in time to keep her from being shipped off to Underwood.

The girls were silent for a moment. Then Barbie put her hand over Chelsie's. "I'm so sorry."

Chelsie nodded. But she didn't cry. She was all out of tears. "I feel like I'm going to miss so much," Chelsie said quietly. "I'll miss you. I'll miss the school. And I'll miss doing all the things I secretly wanted to do."

"Like what?" Ana asked curiously.

Chelsie smiled shyly. "Like wearing something outrageous. Like skating in the park. Like walking down the street feeling good about who you are and how you look and . . . I don't know, being like you guys, I suppose."

The girls looked at each other. Then, one by one, they began to smile.

Tori slapped her hand on the table. "There's one good thing about your situation, mate. You've got nothing to lose. Right?"

"That's true," Chelsie agreed.

"That's all we wanted to know," Tori said with a laugh. She threw Barbie, Ana, Lara, and Nichelle a meaningful look. The four nodded knowingly. Suddenly, as if in response to some invisible signal, the girls rose, and Chelsie found herself being hustled out of the coffee shop like a sheep surrounded by Border collies.

"Where are we going?" Chelsie asked.

"It's Chelsie's dream day," Barbie answered. "First stop, Thrift-O-Rama."

"Oh, no!" Chelsie cried as the girls hustled her around the corner and into the coolest, most outrageous, retro-thrift boutique in Manhattan.

Inside the boutique, the music thundered. Kids gathered around bins full of shoes and hats, watching each other try things on and giving one another good-natured advice and fashion critiques.

"Go look at hats while we cruise for dresses," Barbie instructed, gently shoving her toward a group of kids gathered around a large box of hats.

At first, Chelsie was reluctant to approach the group. From the way they were laughing and talking, they appeared to be old friends.

A cute guy — not too much older than Chelsie, but obviously an employee — caught her eye and waved her over. "Hi!" His greeting was so friendly and unaffected, Chelsie couldn't help but respond.

"Hi!" she answered.

"I'm Dave, the Thrift-O-Rama Hatmeister," he said. "Today is the day we give hats away with any purchase. Or even without a purchase if the hat and the head seem to match. Let's see what I've got for you."

The kids standing around Dave began to applaud, urging Chelsie to step forward. Never had Chelsie felt so acutely self-conscious about her English schoolgirl looks. These kids wore wide jeans and hugely tall platform sneakers. Several had colored streaks in their hair. And two girls wore matching blond fifties diner waitress wigs.

Dave studied her for a moment. Then he reached into the bin and pulled out a very Victorian-looking crushed velvet hat with a wide gold ribbon and an antique rose. "This is you!"

Chelsie eyed the hat. It was so, well, big.

David held up the hat, danced toward Chelsie, and placed it on her head. The girls in the blond wigs began to applaud, and Dave turned Chelsie toward the mirror so she could see her reflection.

Chelsie laughed. The fancy, old-fashioned hat was a bit incongruous over her pleated wool skirt and sweater set.

Nichelle materialized beside her. "It's perfect!" she announced. Before Chelsie could move, Nichelle had thrust a short burgundy crushed-velvet dress under Chelsie's chin so that she could see the effect of the dress and the hat in the mirror.

"Add these and you're a goer," Tori added, placing a pair of heavy platform boots on the floor.

"And this." Barbie hung a beaded antique purse from Chelsie's wrist.

Chelsie gazed in speechless wonder at her reflection in the mirror. In a million years, she would never have the nerve to wear an outfit like this.

*Or would she?*

Half an hour later, the girls were skating down

Fifth Avenue toward Washington Square Park. Chelsie had her burgundy dress gathered in the back like a bustle so she could skate.

The girls made a colorful procession as they threaded their way through the other pedestrians.

Barbie brought up the rear, shooting with her digital video camera, and swooping beside them to capture the fun on film.

"Nutrition break!" Tori announced.

The girls came to a skating stop at the hot dog stand. The vendor spoke no English at all. No French. No German. No Spanish. No Italian. With all the languages the girls spoke, they couldn't find one that worked.

Fortunately, "hot dog with mustard" was an internationally recognized phrase. Five minutes later, the girls were all perched on a low wall outside an apartment building eating hot dogs and watching the traffic go by.

"Do you have any idea what hot dogs are made of?" Ana asked, spreading the mustard more evenly along her dog.

"No. And if you're really my friend, you won't tell me," Tori chirped. "I love these things."

"Me, too," echoed Barbie, taking a large bite.

"Think the Pants Boys will be in the park?" Ana asked.

"They'll be there," Tori said.

"Anybody beside me feel guilty that we're not working on the show?" Nichelle asked.

The girls let out a collective groan.

"It's usually Chelsie who's ragging on us," Tori protested. "Chelsie? Hello?"

But Chelsie's attention was focused on the street where a long black limousine was pulling slowly to a stop at a red light. James was at the wheel.

As the limo idled, James turned and looked out the window. Straight at Chelsie.

Her heart stopped.

In the backseat, she saw her mother's face. She, too, seemed to be looking right at Chelsie.

Chelsie's throat tightened. Uh-oh! She was supposed to be grounded. And here she was sitting on a wall, eating hot dogs off the street, wearing what her mother might describe as a "ridiculous getup," and surrounded by girls her mother would think were "extremely unsuitable."

Her stomach flopped. Would her mother get out

of the car and bustle Chelsie into the backseat like some kind of runaway delinquent?

Her mother continued to stare, her face thoughtful, almost wistful, and then she turned, politely bending her head to hear what was being said to her by another passenger.

*She didn't recognize me!* Chelsie thought happily. *She didn't know it was me!*

"Chelsie!" Nichelle said. "For the fifteenth time. Do you want to go to school and run through some of the numbers?"

"NO WAY!" Chelsie shouted. She jumped off the wall and spun around on her skates. "Today is a day to play. Maybe the only day I'll ever have to play. So let's go! Race you to the park."

"No fair!" Tori yelled. She let out a wild whoop, and Chelsie could hear her skates tearing up the pavement behind her.

The park was rocking. There were two bands wailing away, canceling each other out — but Chelsie didn't care. It was the sweetest music she had ever heard.

Two figures scooted up beside her on skateboards and smiled shyly from beneath their caps.

"Hello, Pants Boys," Chelsie said.

They mumbled their greetings and pointed toward the south corner of the park.

"Lead on," she said, guessing that they wanted her to follow them.

Chelsie followed the Pants Boys toward the south corner. As they neared the perimeter of the park, the noise and gay jangle of the crowd seemed to fade away.

A large group had gathered. Chelsie heard the sound of three voices singing in close harmony to a guitar. The Pants Boys helped Chelsie thread her way through the crowd and to the front, beaming as if they had discovered something wonderful that they were thrilled to share with her.

Chelsie listened to the music, thrilled by the intricate harmony and sensitive lyrics. The group was singing a song about the environment and the tragic loss of species in the rain forest. When the song was over, everyone applauded.

Pants Boy One skated up to the singers and whispered something in the lead performer's ear. The lead performer's eyes scanned the crowd. Pants Boy Two, standing next to Chelsie, began to point at her.

The next thing Chelsie knew, the lead performer

was holding his guitar out to her. "I understand we have an award-winning English songwriter here. Chelsie, would you sing us a song? Please?"

Chelsie felt as if she would rather sink into the ground. But the performer's request was so sincere and polite, and the crowd was applauding with so much enthusiasm, Chelsie could not refuse.

Uncertainly, she stepped forward and accepted the guitar. The Pants Boys quickly turned an empty trash can upside down and boosted her up so that she had a place to sit and balance the guitar.

"Thank you," Chelsie said shyly. "I'd like to sing a new song. A song about . . ." Her voice cracked, and she broke off, feeling suddenly shy and scared.

The singer who had lent her his guitar leaned over and whispered in her ear, "Singing is like kissing. Easier with your eyes closed."

That made Chelsie giggle. She closed her eyes, strummed the guitar, and found the key she wanted. Then she began to sing the song she had been reluctant to share with her friends — "When You're Away."

After the first verse, she could almost *feel* the audience responding. And when she sang the chorus the second time, the trio began to join in — singing along and harmonizing.

Chelsie opened her eyes and saw Nichelle, Tori, Ana, and Lara singing and clapping their hands to the music. Barbie was filming the performance with her video camera.

Before she knew it, the song was over. And the group around her had burst into loud and enthusiastic applause. The Pants Boys whistled and executed tight, ecstatic figure eights.

Chelsie bowed, handed the singer his guitar, and hurried to join her friends. "Bonzer song!" Tori gasped as the girls made their way out of the cheering crowd. "Why haven't we heard that song yet?"

Chelsie hesitated. "I don't know. I suppose because it's sad. And you didn't like my sad songs. You thought they were pretentious. That the experience didn't belong to me."

The girls came to a stop. Barbie took one of Chelsie's hands and squeezed it. "Yes, but this song is about an emotion that does belong to you. And it shows in the writing."

"You've had a tough time of it, haven't you, mate?" Tori said.

Suddenly, the bright yellow beauty of the day

seemed unbearably sad. Soon, she would be half a world away. From her friends. From New York. From her dad.

She felt the familiar lump rise in her throat. But she wasn't going to cry. No. She was not going to cry. The friendly faces surrounding her were so brave and so strong, they gave her courage. Real girls didn't cry. Real girls took action.

# Chapter 10

# A Code Id Da Dose

"Chelsie! Dinner's ready!"

"Coming, Mother!" Chelsie shouted.

"Yikes!" Chelsie shrieked as she caught sight of her reflection in the hall mirror.

She ducked back into her room. Oh, no! What had she been thinking?

"Chelsie!" her mother called again.

"Coming!" Chelsie grabbed her robe and put it on over her outfit.

When she made her entrance into the dining room, her mother looked concerned. "I was afraid of this."

Chelsie's heart missed a beat. "Afraid of what?" she asked.

"I can see you've got a cold." Her mother got up, came over, and put a hand over Chelsie's forehead. "No fever," she murmured.

Chelsie started to argue that she felt fine. But then she swallowed the words. If her mother thought she had a cold, that was a perfect excuse to hide under her robe.

"I'm sorry I was so harsh last night," her mother said softly.

"That's all right," Chelsie said warily, wondering if her mother was working her way up to the boarding school conversation.

Chelsie took her seat and faked a sneeze. Her mother gave her an odd look. "Would you like a decongestant?"

"Maybe after dinner," Chelsie answered.

Two steaming bowls of pumpkin soup were already on the table, and her mother picked up her spoon. As she spooned up the soup, her eyes dropped to her bowl.

Her mother frowned. "I wonder if you should stay home tomorrow."

# Singing Sensation

"NO!" Chelsie cried.

"I don't want you coming down with anything," her mother said, almost to herself. "Not now . . ."

Chelsie held her breath. Of course her mother didn't want her coming down with anything. She was planning to send her back to England on Friday night. If she were sick, she wouldn't be able to fly.

Ah-hah! A lightbulb went off over Chelsie's head.

She began to hack and cough, trying to sound as sick as possible. If she could just manage to be home until her father got here, she could plead with him not to send her away.

"You know," Chelsie said, trying to sound as muffled as possible, "I think I am getting sick. Do you mind if I go lie down?"

Mrs. Peterson shook her head. "Fine. I'll ask Alice to bring you up a tray. Perhaps you'd better stay home from school next week. In fact, I insist upon it. Now, I will be out most of the week, but I want you to stay in bed and make sure that you are perfectly well by next weekend. Understand?"

Chelsie understood. She understood more than her mother dreamed.

But that was okay. One way or another, she'd find a way to make sure *Love What You Do* was a success.

Chelsie was happy to spend Sunday in her room eating meals off a tray. She had a ton of rewriting to do. And having a full, uninterrupted day gave her the extra time she needed.

By Sunday night, she was satisfied that she had done the best job she could possibly do.

The show was, as they say, "frozen." That meant that, as of tomorrow, rehearsals started.

She lay down and snuggled comfortably in her bed.

The next morning, she found a tray on her table with tea and a muffin. Alice must have tiptoed in and left it while Chelsie slept. Chelsie hungrily devoured the muffin and gulped the tea.

She slipped into the bathroom, brushed out her tight braid, and redid her hair in a loose ponytail low on her back. Then she ran into her room, jumped into her velvet dress and, quick as lightning, pulled on a robe just as Mrs. Peterson knocked on the door.

"Come in," Chelsie said.

# Singing Sensation

Mrs. Peterson walked in. "Chelsie," she said. "I'll be in Connecticut most of the day. And I won't be home until this evening. You stay in bed, and I'll ask Alice to look in on you."

"OH, DOH!" Chelsie quickly protested. "Ummmm, I woodin' wan' Alice to catch my code. If she geds sick, who'd make all dose tea sandwiches?"

Her mother blinked. "Is that a joke?"

Chelsie wasn't sure. Maybe. But her mother wasn't known for her great sense of humor. "Do," she said quietly. "I just don't want my sickness to keep you from being able to do your duty."

Her mother blinked again, as if she suspected Chelsie of not being serious.

"I'll be okay. Really. I'd rather get my own food than have Alice waking me up."

That answer seemed to satisfy Mrs. Peterson, and she smiled. "Very well. I'll see you this evening."

As soon as she was gone, Chelsie removed her robe, jumped into her boots, and snuck downstairs. As soon as she heard the front door close, she darted out the back door with her backpack. The subway wasn't far, and Chelsie didn't mind taking it. In fact, she preferred it to the slow and stately limo.

Zip, zip, zip. The subway carried her quickly down to Battery Park. Chelsie entered the I. H. building just as the bell rang.

The first person she saw was Melissa. Melissa reared back, as if totally blown away by Chelsie's new look.

"I was hoping to see you," Chelsie said with a smile. She reached into her backpack, removed the final draft of all the lyrics, and handed them to Melissa. "It's all there."

Barbie saw her, gave her a cheery wave, and came to join them. Moments later, Tori, Ana, Lara, and Nichelle drifted over from their lockers.

"You look bonzer," Tori told Chelsie.

"Mega-bonzer," Nichelle added with a giggle.

"You'll be the queen of I. H.," Barbie said. "Is the new song in there?"

Chelsie nodded. "It's in there."

"Will you sing it yourself?" Ana asked. "Please?"

Chelsie shook her head. "I'm sorry. But my part is finished. I have to go home. It's up to you now. Good luck."

"You mean you're not going to be here for the rehearsals?"

Chelsie forced a smile. "No. I can't. But you'll do fine. You're all wonderful singers and dancers and designers and —" Chelsie couldn't finish. She turned and ran for the exit. Past the lockers. Past the hall that led to the gymnasium. Past the sculptures in the school yard. Past Battery Park. Past the river.

In the distance, Chelsie saw the Statue of Liberty beckoning. If only it could call her father home. Soon. Before it was too late.

# Chapter 11

# Cards on the Table

**B**y Thursday, Chelsie was a nervous wreck. She had snuck into the study again. The plane ticket with her name on it was still there. She was still scheduled to take off at 7:30 P.M.

Every time her mother opened her mouth to speak, Chelsie was certain she was going to say something about Underwood and returning to England.

But she didn't. Waiting for the ax to fall was driving Chelsie insane. Besides that, she was totally depressed. Pretending to be sick was worse than really being sick. It was hard to lie in bed all day when you didn't feel bad. Chelsie chewed on a nail, nervously wondering how the rehearsals were going.

Was Blaine playing a believable parrot?

Was Fletcher still tripping over everybody and everything?

Did the singers understand the rhythm of the new lyrics?

And most of all, who was going to sing her song?

Chelsie paced nervously around her room. Finally, she couldn't stand being cooped up anymore.

She slipped on her robe and padded softly down the steps. Her mother was sitting in the window seat in the front hall, looking out at the rain. The expression on her face was as melancholy as Chelsie's mood.

"When is Daddy coming home?" Chelsie asked.

Her mother leaned her head against her hand. "I don't know. Soon, I hope." Her voice was weary. And sad.

Suddenly, Chelsie understood something.

Her mother was missing her father. Missing him as much as Chelsie did. Maybe more. A whole new vista of thought opened up. Maybe Mr. Peterson was the only one who really understood her mother. Maybe when he was gone, her mother felt just as lonely and abandoned as Chelsie.

"He's negotiating a trade agreement. A very important trade agreement that will affect a lot of people. We have to let him do his job."

Usually, when her mother said things like that, Chelsie felt as if she were being lectured. She felt as if she were somehow at fault for missing Mr. Peterson. But now, she saw that her mother was not lecturing Chelsie about what she should or shouldn't feel, she was lecturing *herself*.

"You miss him, don't you?" Chelsie asked.

"Every minute of every day," her mother answered with a soft smile, turning her face toward Chelsie. "But I have to let him be what he is. That's how I show him that I love him."

Suddenly, Chelsie saw that the formality her father showed her mother was not formality at all. It was respect. And love. It was the way he signaled his affection for her.

With Chelsie, he was different. He teased her, laughed with her, and listened to her songs. That was how he demonstrated his love for his daughter.

As she watched her mother's face, Chelsie saw

Mrs. Peterson's soft smile turn slowly to an astonished, openmouthed gape. "Chelsie Peterson," she gasped. "*What* are you wearing?"

Chelsie let out a little shriek of surprise. Her robe had opened, revealing her velvet dress.

Her mother jumped to her feet. "Have you really been sick, or has this cold-in-the-nose business simply been a ruse to keep me from seeing that you were hiding something?"

"Yes, I have been hiding something," Chelsie cried angrily. "But I'm not the only one. When, exactly, were you planning to tell me about Underwood?"

Her mother closed her eyes as if she were in pain.

"I saw the letter," Chelsie shouted in an accusatory tone. "I saw the ticket. I'm leaving tomorrow. Aren't I?"

Her mother didn't answer.

"Aren't I?" Chelsie shouted.

"Yes! No! I don't know," her mother said in quick succession. "I mean, I haven't decided yet. I can still cancel the ticket."

"Why didn't you tell me about this?" Chelsie demanded.

"Because — because sometimes it's better not to have too much time to fret over things. Sometimes it's better just to have someone take the decision out of your hands. You will be happier at Underwood," she said, trying to keep her voice steady.

"No, I won't!" Chelsie protested. "I want to stay here. Does Daddy know?" She was crying now. Choking on her tears.

Her mother swallowed. "I had hoped your father would be home in time for me to discuss this with him. But since he cannot come home, I am going to have to make this decision myself."

"Then he doesn't know?" Chelsie sobbed, torn between anger and relief.

Her mother shook her head. "No. But he wants you to be happy. And so do I."

"Do I look happy?" Chelsie demanded, groping for the tissue that she needed now for real.

Her mother shook her head. "No," she said softly. "But you will."

"Mrs. Peterson?"

Alice hovered uncertainly in the doorway. "James is ready to take you to the Irish Delegation."

"Thank you, Alice," Mrs. Peterson said. "I'll be leaving soon. Would you help Chelsie pack her bags? She will be going back to England tomorrow night."

Chelsie twirled around and ran up the stairs.

This was a nightmare. An absolute nightmare.

The phone rang. Chelsie picked it up. Maybe it was her father. "Hello?"

"I know you told me not to call you, mate. But I just had to tell you that the dress rehearsal went great. Melissa Larkin is singing your song. Who knew Ms. Brilliant chess champ and script girl had a voice like an angel? I wish you could hear."

Tori chattered on and on. It was several minutes before she realized that Chelsie wasn't speaking, and was weeping silently into the phone. "Uh-oh! What's wrong?" she asked.

"I'm leaving. I'm leaving tomorrow night. My mother is sending me back to England."

"No! What did your dad say?"

"He doesn't know!" Chelsie choked. "He still doesn't know."

"Then we have to let him know," Tori announced.

"No," Chelsie managed to say in a gruff voice. "I can't. He's busy with things that affect a lot of people and . . ." Chelsie broke off. "Let's not talk about it. I'll write to you. I'll write to you all. Will you write to me and let me know how the show goes? And if we won?"

"We'll win," Tori said confidently. "The dress rehearsal was a total disaster. Mr. Toussaint says that guarantees the show will be a success."

Chelsie let out a watery chuckle. "I'm glad. Break a leg tomorrow."

"Don't you worry," Tori said. "We'll break legs, arms, heads. Whatever it takes. This is an extreme competition, remember?"

"I'll never forget," Chelsie told her friend. "Never."

\* \* \* \*

"Chelsie, do you have your purse?" asked Mrs. Peterson.

"Yes," Chelsie answered softly.

James began carrying Chelsie's suitcases out to the car, and Alice gave Chelsie a quick peck on the cheek. "Good luck to you," she said.

"Thank you," Chelsie said, her throat so tight, she could barely talk.

James opened the door for Chelsie and Mrs. Peterson. Neither said a word as the car began moving downtown. The limo came to a stop at a light right outside Recorded History. Chelsie could see her friend, Peter, inside the shop, putting some CDs on the shelf.

Peter had been a terrific teacher, Chelsie realized. In one lesson, he had taught her things about content and craft that had helped her produce some of the best work she had ever written.

"Mother," Chelsie said. "Excuse me. But I have to run into that shop for just a moment."

"Chelsie!"

Chelsie jumped out of the car and ran into the store. Somehow, she felt she had to let him know that he had touched her life and her career in an important way. She wanted someone in New York to remember that she had been there — and that she had learned something from her visit.

She was just about to call his name when she saw Damian come running in with a couple of his cronies. Chelsie ducked down behind the "Heavy Metal" display. She didn't want Damian to see her.

"I can't believe that Melissa girl had the nerve to go and get laryngitis," she heard Damian say. "That blows the best number in our show."

"So why are we here?" one of his companions asked.

Damian took a small device off the shelf and turned it on. It made a loud and steady clicking sound. "Sabotage by metronome," he explained. "If we hook this baby into an amplifier when the juniors do their precision tap number, it'll completely confuse their rhythm. That's their best number. If they blow it, we've got a pretty good chance of winning."

The other boy began to laugh. "Damian, you're a genius."

Chelsie felt hot and cold at the same time. This was horrible. Somebody had to do something. But who?

Chelsie ran outside and rapped at her mother's window.

Her mother put the window down. "Chelsie," she began. "Come on. We have to —"

"Mother," she said breathlessly. "I know you're not going to understand. But you know how you're always talking about duty and responsibility? Well, I have a duty, too. And responsibilities. Right now, my show is in trouble. I'm the only one who can fix it. I'll meet you at the airport. Word of honor. Wait for me there."

"But, Chelsie," protested her mother, "you're supposed to check in at —"

But Chelsie didn't wait to hear the rest. She ran toward I. H. as if her life depended on it.

# Chapter 12

# A Little Help from My Friends

C helsie ran past the garbage cans that were always stacked beside the side door of the school, near the auditorium.

As soon as she was inside, she could hear the music playing in the auditorium. It sounded like SING OUT! was well under way.

She looked left and right, hoping she'd beaten Damian to school.

"*Allo!* Chelsie! You came!" Lara was shoving a huge piece of scenery down the hallway toward the backstage area. She left the scenery and ran to give Chelsie a hug.

"We've got a problem," Chelsie panted. Quickly, she told Lara what she had heard.

"*Oooh-lala!* This is bad," Lara said. "Not to worry. I think I know what to do." Lara put two fingers to her lips and whistled, as if for a taxi.

Right on cue, the Pants Boys came skidding around the corner on skateboards.

"They decided they would rather be my assistants than perform," Lara explained to Chelsie. Then she turned to the Pants Boys, and in some language understood only by the three of them, they discussed what to do about Damian's rotten plot.

"Here he comes now," Chelsie breathed.

Damian came striding in the doors, looking as if he owned the place — which was exactly what you might expect from the principal's son.

*ZZZZZZzzzzzzz!* The Pants Boys' skateboards skidded along the linoleum floor.

Quick as lightning, they reached out, and each one grabbed Damian by the arm.

"Hey!" Damian yelled as the Pants Boys lifted him off his feet and carried him out the door at top speed.

*KABOOM! CRASH! CHING!!!*

"Sounds like they dumped him in the trash cans," Lara said with a smile. "Good. That problem is solved. Now you must solve another."

"I know," Chelsie said. "Melissa can't sing. So I have to. Right?"

"That is right. Come on. Let's get Nichelle so she can fix your costume."

Chelsie hurried backstage. Tori, Nichelle, Barbie, and Ana all ran to greet her. But there wasn't much time for talking or hugging. They had work to do.

The order of the performances had been chosen by lot. The seniors had gone on first, followed by the freshmen. Onstage now, the juniors were presenting their finale, which featured Jo Jo and Kingsley's breathtakingly professional tap and hip-hop number. The audience was roaring its approval.

"Come on," Nichelle said. "I can let out the hem of Melissa's costume. But it'll take some time. Marina, will you help everybody else get dressed?"

Marina nodded.

Out in the auditorium, the audience of students, parents, and teachers had erupted into applause. The juniors' SING OUT! performance was over.

And they had done well. Now it was time for the sophomores to go on.

Nichelle was pumped up. "Okay, everybody — it's show time!" she exhorted. "Time to show everyone what we can do!"

For Chelsie, the next fifteen minutes went by in a blur. She tried to sit still and stay calm while someone made up her face, combed out her hair, and fitted her costume around her. But she knew that her classmates were out there performing their hearts out. And she also knew that she would soon be out there, too, singing the showstopping number that she hoped would give the sophomores a winning edge over the juniors.

Suddenly, it was time. She was on.

"Go!" Tori urged, pushing her onstage. "Go now!"

Chelsie looked at her watch. She had just enough time to sing her song, jump back into her clothes, catch a taxi, and meet her mother at the airport.

The lights hit her.

She was blinded for a moment, but as soon as she lifted her chin and began to sing "When You're Away," she forgot her nervousness and her fears.

The crowded auditorium hushed as she sang.

Even to her own ears, her voice sounded clear and angelic. Never had she sung so well. Never had she felt so sincere about what she was singing.

When the song was over, she held the last note, and then closed her eyes and lifted her arms, embracing the applause that thundered around her, shaking the stage beneath her feet.

Chelsie bowed, then ran offstage.

Barbie and Lara had tears running down their cheeks. Tori was grinning from ear to ear, and Nichelle and Ana were pumping their fists.

"You're a smash hit!" Tori said. "Go take a bow."

"I don't have time," Chelsie protested. "I don't have time. I have to go."

"Now?" Barbie cried.

"Yes, now," Chelsie answered.

Then, suddenly, the girls were in each others' arms. All of them crying. All of them hugging.

"Crikey, I'll miss you," Tori choked, wiping her nose on her sleeve.

"We'll all miss you," Barbie said.

"I'll miss you, too," Chelsie said. She turned and drew in her breath with a gasp.

Behind her . . . watching the scene . . . was Mrs. Peterson. And there was someone else. Someone in a raincoat and a hat. Someone who looked very much like . . .

"DADDY!" Chelsie cried, running toward him.

Mr. Peterson gathered Chelsie in his arms and spun her around. "I am so proud of you!"

"What are you doing here?" she asked. "How did you know?"

Mr. Peterson put Chelsie down and walked toward Barbie, Tori, Ana, Lara, and Nichelle. "I think you can thank these girls, who are, if I am not mistaken, your friends?"

Mrs. Peterson's mouth opened slightly. "Friends?" she repeated.

The girls exchanged shamefaced glances.

"Got a confession, mate," Tori said. "Yesterday, after we spoke, we decided to take matters into our own hands. We knew you needed your old man to come back. So we got him back."

"Indeed, they did," Mr. Peterson said, giving her friends an appreciative nod. "First, they went to my office and got my e-mail address from my secretary. Then they sent me a most interesting digital video. This new technology is amazing, I must say. Barbie shot the video, I understand, and Tori mailed it to me over the Internet. Imagine my surprise to see my very own Chelsie singing that beautiful, touching song. And she was also writing happy songs, cutting up like a class clown, and skating around town in a very fetching dress. Surely you can understand that this behavior is so out of character, so odd, so unprecedented, that I just had to fly back and see for myself whether or not this girl on the video was indeed my Chelsie."

"It's me," Chelsie admitted, dropping her eyes and hoping that he wasn't too disappointed in her.

"I'm so glad your father was able to reach me in time," said Mrs. Peterson. "He got me on the car phone, and I turned right around and came back. He was already on his way here in a taxi."

"I think we'd better clear out and give you folks some privacy," Tori said to the other girls. "Come on, mates."

"Are you angry?" Chelsie asked her parents meekly.

"Oh, Chelsie!" her father said, "Why didn't you tell us? We've both been so worried about you."

"Tell you what? I don't understand."

"We thought you had no friends," Mrs. Peterson said. "We were afraid you were having a rather hard time fitting in. All those sad songs concerned us. Here you were in the biggest playground in the world, and you seemed completely isolated and unhappy."

Chelsie turned toward her father and said, "I was only sad because you're always gone. I know I'm not supposed to resent it. But I do."

Her mother put an arm around Chelsie's shoulder. "Of course you do. I did, too, when I was your age — when my father wasn't there for me. Sometimes I think this diplomatic life is too hard on families. The constant moving. The difficulty in making new friends. That's why I thought you would be happier at Underwood. Better able to fit in."

"Why didn't you tell me?" Chelsie asked.

"When I was your age, I always felt that I didn't fit in because there was something wrong with me," Mrs. Peterson explained. "And I always felt that my parents were disappointed in me because I wasn't able to cope. I never wanted you to feel that way. It's a horrible feeling. It was better to let you think that we simply wanted you there for reasons of tradition and safety."

"But why didn't you tell me sooner?" Chelsie asked.

"Because I didn't want to add to your worries before I had to. I felt you'd be much better off in England, but I didn't know if you would see that. And now I see that I was wrong. You are really happy here, and you do have some lovely friends who care about you."

Chelsie threw her arms around her mother. "Oh, I am happy here," she cried. "I'm so sorry you worried about me." She gave her mother a big hug, realizing now how much she had been suffering, too, trying to decide on the right thing to do. "Why don't we explore New York together?" she said. "If Daddy can come, great. If not, we'll have fun together."

Mrs. Peterson laughed and tightened her arms around Chelsie.

"Chelsie! Chelsie!"

Barbie, Tori, Nichelle, Ana, and Lara came running over. "Come on! They're about to announce the winners."

Mrs. Peterson gently pushed Chelsie toward the girls. "Go. Go with your friends."

Mr. and Mrs. Peterson both lifted their hands to

show Chelsie that they had their fingers crossed for good luck.

Principal Simmons walked onto the stage and held up her hands. "Quiet, please. Quiet! The votes are in! The winner of the first I. H. SING OUT! is . . . THE SOPHOMORE CLASS! It was a very tough call between the sophs and the juniors, but the judges felt that the sophomores' fine song-writing and superior acting gave them the edge. Take a bow, sophomores!"

The entire cast and crew came pouring out onto the stage. They hugged, they high-fived, and they swung each other around in gleeful circles.

"Uh-oh!" Tori shouted, pointing her finger. "Look, Barbie. I think you've lost your boyfriend."

Over in a dark corner of the stage, Fletcher and Melissa were snuggling.

Barbie just smiled. She was genuinely happy for Fletcher.

"What in the world do they have in common?" Nichelle wondered.

"I know," Tori said with a grin. "They're both extreme. He's extremely tall; she's extremely short. He's extremely clumsy; she's extremely organized. They're the extreme couple. What d'ya think?"

"I don't know," Chelsie answered with a gurgling laugh. "All I know is that right now, I am extremely happy and . . . *whoaaaaa!*"

Suddenly, Chelsie found herself lifted up on the shoulders of the cast members of the sophomore class. She raised her arms over her head in a gesture of triumph. And from her perch on the top of the world, she could look down and see the future — which was full of fun, friendship, love, and a million Manhattan adventures with Barbie and her other great friends.

# BORIS 'POOGY' PUGACHOV: FROM RUSSIA TO INTERNATIONAL HIGH SCHOOL

If your locker door has ever jammed or you've lost your book bag, then you have probably met Boris "Poogy" Pugachov. Mr. Pugachov is the custodian here at International High. Poogy describes his job as a little bit of everything. He fixes anything that is broken, cleans up messes, and runs the lost-and-found.

In an interview last week, Poogy described the life that he left in Russia, where he was an architect. Poogy has always wanted to come to America, and had the opportunity to move to New York City recently. He is working very hard and saving his money so that he can bring the rest of his family over to this country.

Poogy loves International High and its students and is very excited about the new building.

# GATHERING INFORMATION

The purpose of a news article is to inform the reader. However, before any information can be passed along, the author must research the topic he or she is writing about. There are many ways to do this.

• The interview is one of the most common ways for a journalist to gather information about a person or an event. The article about Poogy is based on an interview and is full of information that could not have been found anywhere other than from Mr. Pugachov.

• Personal observation is appropriate for an article about a sporting event or a performance.

 • If you needed to find out about current events, there are many excellent Internet web sites devoted to news.

**To write a news article:**

Whenever you are researching an article, it is very important to be prepared: Do your homework. If you are interviewing a person, prepare a list of questions before you start. Try some of the following ideas to help you get started:

• Choose a person to interview for practice. For your first inter- view, choose some- one you know well. This will help you to feel comfortable.

• Prepare a list of questions. Think about what makes this person special. Is the person an excellent student or a gifted musician? Focus on the person's talents.

• Meet with this person and ask your questions. Listen carefully and take notes. Try to include as much information in your notes as possible, as you will be using them to write your article.

• After you write the article, ask a friend to read
it. Did your friend learn
something new about the
subject of your interview?
(Remember, your goal is to
inform other people.)

Remember: **WRITING=HONESTY=TRUTH**